First published in Belgium and Holland by Clavis Uitgeverij, Hasselt – Amsterdam, 2017
Copyright © 2017, Clavis Uitgeverij

English translation from the Dutch by Clavis Publishing Inc. New York
Copyright © 2017 for the English language edition: Clavis Publishing Inc. New York

Visit us on the web at www.clavisbooks.com

It's My Birthday written and illustrated by Liesbet Slegers
Original title: Ik ben jarig
Translated from the Dutch by Clavis Publishing

ISBN 978-1-60537-345-4

This book was printed in January 2017 at Wai Man Book Binding (China) Ltd. Flat A, 9/F., Phase 1, Kwun Tong Industrial Centre, 472-484 Kwun Tong Road, Kwun Tong, Kowloon, H.K.

First Edition
10 9 8 7 6 5 4 3 2 1

It's My Birthday

Liesbet Slegers

Clavis
NEW YORK

I yawn and wake up
in my cozy little bed.
I slept really well.

Good morning!

I take off my pajamas
and put on my clothes.
I get to wear a crown today!
Hooray!

What's that in
the living room?
A box full of **banners**.
What should I do with
these banners?

I hang the banners
on the wall.
How nice they look!
It's a party!

This is my house.
I have a dog and a cat.
There is a mailbox in
front of the house.
But... why am I wearing
that **crown** on my head?

It's my **birthday!**
I decorate the front of
the house with banners
and balloons. Now everyone
can tell there's a party
at my place.

I look out the window.
When will the guests **arrive?**
Waiting is hard....
Who will come to my party?

Hello, Rose!
Hello, **Grandma and Grandpa!**
I am glad you came!

I get lots of **presents**.
I like getting presents!
What's inside the packages?

I love unwrapping presents!
Rose gives me blocks.
I get a **panda bear**
from my Grandma.

Mommy brings in a **big cake.**
It's a real birthday cake
with candles on top.
The candles are burning. I blow....

I blew out the **candles!**
Everybody is clapping and singing.
Having a birthday party is fun!